THE DAY THE WORLD WENT INSIDE

A story of hope and triumph
during challenging times

Written by: Gail Henry-Daniels
Illustrated by: Jeffrey Scott Perdziak

Archway Publishing books may be ordered through booksellers or by contacting:

Archway Publishing
1663 Liberty Drive
Bloomington, IN 47403
www.archwaypublishing.com
844.669.3957

Because of the dynamic nature of the Internet, any web addresses or links contained in this book may have changed since publication and may no longer be valid. The views expressed in this work are solely those of the author and do not necessarily reflect the views of the publisher, and the publisher hereby disclaims any responsibility for them.

Any people depicted in stock imagery provided by Getty Images are models, and such images are being used for illustrative purposes only. Certain stock imagery © Getty Images.

ISBN: 978-1-4808-9688-8 (sc)
ISBN: 978-1-4808-9533-1 (e)

Print information available on the last page.

Archway Publishing rev. date: 10/29/2020

The Day the World Went Inside is dedicated to my loving family. Thank you for daily inspirations, and for the love and joy we share today, tomorrow, and always.

To Mom and Dad for teaching me to have the confidence to just be myself, and for their steadfast example of kindness and love.

A portion of the proceeds from the sale of *The Day the World Went Inside* will be donated to **Steven's Spirit of Giving**/a 501c3 nonprofit organization whose mission is to promote kindness, good deeds and volunteerism in our communities by helping those in need.

We wish to share our sincere gratitude to those friends and supporters who make it possible for us to continue the good works of Steven's Spirit.

The Day the World Went Inside story was inspired by the initial fears of the author's grandchildren during the Covid 19 pandemic. As with most things in life, if you look hard enough even difficult and challenging times have positive lessons. After each dark cloud you can find the beautiful silver lining that teaches us, we have the power to make the world a better place for ourselves and others.

About the Author:

Western New York based author Gail Henry-Daniels has always had a passion for books. Whether reading or writing...she feels the written story has the power to take us places we may never otherwise go and teach us things we may not otherwise know.

Gail holds a M.S. in Higher Education Administration and a B.S. in Human and Community Service. She has over 30 years work experience in the education arena, including 20 years managing a child and family wellbeing-based research program. In 2017 she received a Humanitarian of the Year Award for her volunteer efforts helping elementary school children's programs.

Gail is founder and serves as president of the 501c3 nonprofit organization *Steven's Spirit of Giving* Inc. formed in memory of her son Steven.

About the Illustrator:

Jeff has always been an artist. Ever since he can remember he has been creating reality on paper with his pencils. Jeff has completed many different projects over the years. Pencil portraits to a life size painting of a train on the side of a bowling alley, namely the West Shore Railway mural in Clarence, New York.

Jeff's talents bring him to work on wildlife art for local animal rehabilitation groups, t-shirt designs for artists like Carrie Underwood and BB King, more than half a dozen children's books and many murals with his favorite works...superhero art!

You can catch up with all of Jeff's work on social media.

One day in the town of Sunnydale, the sun did not shine.

The sun had shone every day for 100 years in the town of Sunnydale...

...but that day there was no sun to be found!

The children looked out the window of their houses and rubbed their eyes in surprise at what they did not see!

They cried out, "Mommy, Daddy! Where did the sun go?"

"The world must be changing," said their parents.
"We better stay inside!"

Out in the forest, Rian Rabbit noticed the sun was not shining. He began to worry, so he hopped over to tell Stevie Squirrel.

"The sun is not shining, the sun is not shining! Oh, my!" exclaimed Stevie Squirrel as he peaked out of his tree house.

"The world must be changing! We better warn our friends!" Then they scampered off to tell Blue Jay and Blue Jay flew off to tell the other birds.

As Rian Rabbit and Stevie Squirrel scurried on their way to find Freddie Fox, Markie Mallard, Timmy Turtle and Ryleigh Raccoon...

...they saw people wearing masks covering their faces, and no one was walking together! They also noticed that schools, stores, and office buildings were closed, and parking lots were empty.

"The world is really changing!" exclaimed Ryleigh Raccoon!

People young and old became sad.

The sun is not shining, the sun is not shining,
they said to the masked people, there must
be something in the air!

As Rian Rabbit, Ryleigh Raccoon, Freddie Fox, Stevie Squirrel and Blue Jay hopped, ran, scampered, and flew off to tell more friends, they started to notice something different.

Families were spending time together! Through the windows they could see brothers and sisters, moms and dads were laughing together, playing games, cooking, and eating meals together! "The world is really changing," said Rian Rabbit. He began to feel better!

The people of Sunnydale were frightened, and grandparents missed seeing their grandchildren, but good things were happening too!

As the animal friends traveled around the town of Sunnydale, they saw the masked people donating food to those in need.

As they passed food stores filled with masked shoppers, first responders whizzing past on firetrucks...

...and hospitals, they saw heroes rushing to work so they could help others.

Rian Rabbit, his friends and the people of Sunnydale started to be full of hope that the sun would shine again one day!

The citizens of Sunnydale were hoping, and many were praying the air would clear so they could come out of their houses, take off their masks and spend time with friends and neighbors again.

Everyone began to feel the world was changing one good deed at a time.

They saw people showing kindness towards strangers, saying thank you and being grateful for their many blessings, for each other, and for the planet earth.

Finally, one day as if the sky began to smile, the sun began to shine. The air was clear!

People came out of their houses to spend time with neighbors and friends. They were not sad, and Rian Rabbit was not worried any longer.

Love and kindness spread throughout the lands and indeed the world had changed!

Printed in the United States
By Bookmasters